QUEEN OF THE
SILVER
ARROW

For Robert Muchamore and Sophie McKenzie

First published in 2016 in Great Britain by
Barrington Stoke Ltd
18 Walker Street, Edinburgh, EH3 7LP

www.barringtonstoke.co.uk

Text © 2016 Caroline Lawrence

A CIP catalogue record for this book is available
from the British Library upon request

ISBN: 978-1-78112-526-7

Printed in China by Leo

QUEEN OF THE SILVER ARROW

CAROLINE LAWRENCE

1

THE BABY ON THE SPEAR

A King ran through a forest, with a bronze spear in his right hand and a baby girl in his left.

His breath came in great gasps. His chest moved in and out like a blacksmith's bellows. There was spit on his beard and the armpits of his purple robe were dark with sweat. His scarlet cloak flapped behind him and his crown of golden leaves fell off. He did not stop for it.

The baby girl was his daughter, Princess Camilla.

She giggled, for it seemed to her that this was some game.

But it was not a game.

The King was running for his life. He was running for *her* life.

The trees in that part of the forest were cork oaks. Workers had been peeling off the bark when a sudden storm sent them looking for shelter. Curved strips of bark still lay upon the ground.

The King almost tripped on one. As he fell forward, an arrow whined over his head like an angry wasp.

Some god or goddess was protecting him.

Ahead and to his left, he heard the boom of rushing water. It was the river that ran along the border of his land. He turned and plunged into the bushes.

A dozen heartbeats later, the King came out of the bushes and skidded to a halt.

Usually he could splash across the river. But the sudden storm had made it a foamy torrent, bursting its banks.

On the other side, an ancient forest promised a thousand thickets and caves for them to hide in.

Alone, the King might have been able to swim across. But not with a baby under one arm.

The King saw a curved piece of cork bark lying at the foot of a tree, and he had an idea.

He used the bands of linen cloth that swaddled his baby girl to tie her to the strong shaft of his spear. Next he wrapped the curving curl of cork around her. When that was done, he made it all secure with his belt.

Princess Camilla looked like a larva in a cork cocoon.

The enemy was almost upon them. The King lifted the spear, heavy with the squirming baby, and shouted a prayer to the heavens.

"Diana," he cried, "Goddess of the Hunt! Show mercy to me. I am King Metabus, the father of this baby, Camilla. If you protect her as she flies to you, I vow she will serve you for ever!"

Then he hurled the spear – and with it his child – across the river.

2

ACCA

My name is Acca. I live in Laurentum, a town to the south of the River Tiber.

When I was little, my father used to tell me the story of the baby girl on the spear.

He told me how her father swam across the torrent, and when he rose gasping out of the river and ran to her, the spear was stuck fast in the ground. Baby Camilla was swaying back and forth and giggling. She still thought that it was a game!

My father was a woodcutter. Every morning he went into the woods with an axe and our faithful donkey. If he returned early, he smelled of oak. If he came home at dusk, he smelled of the blue pine higher in the mountains. Sometimes he took his bow and arrows. Those nights we feasted on rabbits or game birds.

I, his daughter, wanted to be like him. My little brother wanted to weave wool at the loom like my mother.

Once, when I was almost five, I asked my father, "Why can't girls hunt and boys weave wool?"

"They can," he said, "but the gods must approve."

That was when he first told me about baby Camilla. He told me how her father, King Metabus, kept his vow. He raised his daughter in a cave in the woods with furs for a bed and wild honey for food. As soon as she could walk, he showed her how to hunt and how to honour the goddess Diana.

"Did Camilla live long ago?" I asked my father one night as he was tucking me into bed.

He looked surprised. "No," he said. "She's alive right now. She's your age."

"Where?" I cried. "Where is she?"

My father leaned close and whispered, "Nobody knows where they live, but I saw her one day when I was cutting wood. She carried a little javelin. And she wore the skin of a tiger cub."

I clapped my hands. "I want a tiger skin, too!"

My father laughed and shook his head.

But for my 5th birthday he gave me a cloak of deer skin, painted with tiger stripes. And a toy bow and arrow.

Any time I was not at the loom, I pretended to be Camilla. I learned to ride our donkey, more stubborn than any horse. I practised every day with my bow and arrows.

But then, when I was ten, my father and little brother both died of a fever. The same illness took many others in our town, among them the only son of our King and Queen. Now King Latinus and Queen Amata had only a daughter, Princess Lavinia.

From that time on, I stopped pretending and learned to hunt for real. I had to help put food on our table now.

I hunted rabbits and birds with my father's bow and arrows.

I hated to kill, and I only did it to feed myself and my mother.

But I loved to be alone in the woods. They were silent and sun-dappled, and I hoped that I might meet Camilla there.

One day I saw a young deer, with antlers that were just beginning to show on top of his head. I had never killed such a big animal before. He would feed us for a month! I could sell his skin! But just as I was about to let my arrow fly, I noticed a garland of flowers around his neck.

Amazed, I followed the stag back to a hut outside the town walls.

That was how I met Silvia, the daughter of the King's herdsman. She was my age and the stag was her pet.

Silvia became my friend, and so did her four little brothers. They helped their father watch the King's cattle.

Almo, the eldest of Silvia's brothers, had seen Camilla running across a field. She held a hunting spear, he said. She was so fast that the grass barely moved beneath her feet.

Every day I looked for her.

I was sixteen when reports first came to us that the Trojans were coming. They had lived in a city called Troy, far to the east. The Greeks had beaten them in a famous war.

For seven years they had been seeking a new homeland.

And now they were on their way here!

King Latinus had a dream that if he married his daughter to a prince from a distant land, his kingdom would become the greatest on earth.

But Queen Amata said the Trojans were barbarians and pirates. She wanted Lavinia to marry her nephew Turnus, the prince of a nearby town and a Latin like us.

Our men and boys were excited by the possibility of a battle. They worked night and day to improve their warcraft in a field outside the town walls. They threw javelins and rode their chariots back and forth. They practised boxing and archery. They called this work their "War Games".

Almo and I hardened oak in the fire and used it to make our own javelins. We tossed them at bales of hay. Silvia was too gentle to fight, but she liked to sit with her pet stag and watch us.

Then a rumour reached us that Camilla had taken to dressing as an Amazon, a female warrior. They said she rode a great black horse. They said she carried a golden bow and silver arrows. They said she wore a little purple cape and a short white tunic with one breast exposed!

When the girls of Laurentum heard this rumour, they began to wear little coloured capes and short white tunics. Some even started carrying golden bows and painted quivers. But none of them dared to expose one breast.

Three of the richest girls learned to ride. Their names were Tulla, Larina and Tarpeia, or Tarpi for short. Like me, they were sixteen and would soon be married, but their parents allowed them to join in the War Games.

They could play at hunting – I had to do it to stay alive.

Still, I admired them for, like me, they wanted to be Camilla.

3

TWO RACES BECOME ONE

Messengers flocked to us like black crows – the Trojans were near!

Their ships had dropped anchor at the mouth of the River Tiber, only five miles north.

They were marching to Laurentum!

Did they mean to fight?

"No," the messengers said. They were not armed. They wished to ask a favour.

A hundred of their warriors came at dusk, with gifts for King Latinus.

The boys stopped their War Games to stare at them.

We girls and women ran up onto the town wall to look down at them.

The most important of our men and women hurried out of the town gates to meet them.

The Trojans were young, handsome and tall. But their dress was so strange. Silvia and I giggled at the floppy caps on their heads.

"They wear long-sleeved tunics and leggings, like girls!" Almo scoffed. "I could take any one of them!"

"Which one is their leader?" a girl asked. It was fair-haired Tulla, one of the rich girls who played at the War Games. She and her friend Tarpi stood next to me on the wall. They wore short white tunics with little blue capes.

Tarpi was stocky with dark, frizzy hair. "I don't think he's there," she said. "My father thinks he must be at least forty. All those men look young."

Their friend Larina ran up. She was the prettiest of the three, and wore a rose-pink cape over her white tunic. "They say King Latinus is going to give the Trojans a feast and soft beds to sleep in," she cried. "They say King Latinus has promised to marry Princess Lavinia to their leader. And he will give them some land near by. Our two races will mix to become one."

"Turnus will be angry," Tulla said.

"Yes!" pretty Larina cried. "He's betrothed to Lavinia!"

"They never announced it," Tarpi said. "Not officially."

Larina gasped at a sudden idea. "Turnus could marry Camilla!" she said. "With her golden bow and arrows. And one breast exposed," she added with a wicked smile.

I could not stay quiet any longer. "Camilla will never marry," I said. "She's devoted to the goddess Diana. And which of you has seen her dressed as an Amazon?"

The three girls looked at me. They were rich and I was poor, but they knew who I was. They were polite because I was standing beside Silvia, whose father watched the King's cattle.

Larina smiled. "Everyone knows Camilla dresses as an Amazon," she said.

"With golden bow and silver arrows," Tarpi said.

"On a great black horse with a gold bridle," Tulla added.

I put my hands on my hips and glared at them. "Who is 'everyone'?" I asked. "Have any of you seen her?"

Larina looked down her nose at me. "No. Have you?"

My voice felt thick. "My father saw her. She wore the skin of a tiger. And she carried a javelin."

"That was when she was little," Tarpi said.

"Ten years ago," Larina said.

"And your father is dead," Tulla pointed out.

Tears pressed the back of my eyes but I would not let them come.

"Who among us has seen her?" I demanded.

They did not reply.

The next day our Trojan guests rode out of Laurentum on a hundred horses from the royal stables. Old King Latinus had got his wish – Lavinia was to wed the Trojan leader and our two races would become one.

4

THE FESTIVAL OF FLOWERS

The Trojans went back to their leader with promises of land and a royal marriage. Three days later we celebrated the Festival of the Flowers.

It was the custom for us unmarried girls to put flowers in our hair, wear our brightest tunics and march from the town to the Hill of Pluto. Then we would welcome the Girl Goddess back from the Underworld with a sacrifice, songs and feasting.

I had traded twenty rabbit pelts for a few feet of leaf-green silk. My mother made it into a beautiful tunic with long sleeves. I planned to walk with Silvia, but her pet stag had gone missing and she was looking for him. So I took up the rear on my own.

Fair-haired Larina and dark-haired Tarpi walked in front of me in their white tunics and blue capes. Like me, they wore garlands of crocus and daffodil on their heads.

"Queen Amata is furious," I heard Tarpi say. "She says the King must be mad to promise their daughter to a man they have never met. She claims he is a Trojan pirate!"

"And Turnus is so brave and handsome." Larina sighed. "Any girl would want to marry him."

"Also," Tarpi pointed out, "Turnus is the Queen's nephew."

"I wish the Trojan leader would marry Camilla," Larina said. "Then Turnus could marry Lavinia and be our King."

"My father says if the Queen has her way then it will come to war," Tarpi whispered, "Turnus will join with us to fight the Trojans."

We were on a path that runs close to the oak woods when something caught my eye.

A girl about my age was standing as still as a deer in the dappled shade of the woods.

She wore no tiger skin. She carried no bow and arrows. But I knew who she was.

"Camilla!" I cried.

The girls in front of me turned to look.

"Where?" Larina squealed. "Where is Princess Camilla?"

"There!" I said, and I smiled at the girl.

"It can't be," said Tarpi.

"Where is her white tunic and purple cape?" Larina asked.

"And her golden quiver?" That was Tarpi.

"She looks like a beggar," said Larina.

"She doesn't look brave," Tarpi scoffed. "She looks scared."

They were right. The girl looked like a frightened beggar.

And yet I knew it was Camilla.

She wore a dirty scarlet tunic and the skin of a black bear as a cloak. She had smeared her pale face with berry juice to make her cheeks pink. Her eyes were swollen from weeping. She wore cow horns in her tangled brown hair, like an old lady.

Larina giggled. "She looks like a cow!"

"She looks ridiculous!" Tarpi's words were loud.

Camilla flinched, as if she had been struck. Her swollen eyes blazed with anger and I saw her make her hands into fists.

"Don't listen to them, Princess Camilla," I said. "We've been waiting for you." Then I smiled at her and held out my hand.

5

THE GIRL IN THE WOODS

Almost all the girls were pointing at Camilla and laughing.

"Silence!" the priest cried from the front of the line. He had not noticed the girl in the woods. "You will alarm the bull. There will be time for dancing and laughter after the sacrifice."

The girls obeyed and began to walk again.

Again, I beckoned the girl to come. "Please," I said. "Please join us."

After a moment, she stepped out of the dappled woods.

"My name is Acca," I whispered.

"I am Camilla," she said, in the accent of a high-born girl.

I took her hand – it was dry and dirty. She was not at all what I imagined.

But how could I be disappointed? She was the baby on the spear! The toddler in the tiger skin!

"Acca, why were the other girls laughing at me?" she whispered, as we fell into step at the rear.

I chose careful words. "You must never wear red or black to the festival," I said. "Those are the colours of blood and death. They belong to Pluto, who stole the Girl Goddess. Also, your hair is done up like an old woman's. And the stains on your cheeks are too red."

Camilla looked down at her grimy bare feet as they moved along the path. "My father once told me that is how his mother wore her hair," she said. "I wish I had a green silk tunic like yours, but all I have is this. It is made from my father's cloak."

"Where is your father?" I asked her.

"Dead." She was still looking down. "He died last week and I burned his body in the sacred grove."

"That is why you have been weeping?"

She nodded. "He never let me join the Festival when he was alive. But I used to watch you from the woods."

I gave her hand a squeeze. "My father died, too," I said. "When I was ten. He taught me to ride and to hunt," I added.

"You ride and hunt?" Her eyebrows went up. "My father told me the girls of Latium do not do those things."

"Most of us do not," I said. "But I do. And some girls play War Games because ..." I was going to say, "Because they want to be like you." Instead I said, "In case we have to fight the Trojans."

"Trojans?" she said.

I nodded. "Did your father tell you about the Greeks and the Trojans?"

"Yes," she said. "He told me stories of a great war in a faraway land. It lasted ten years and only ended when some of the Greeks hid in a hollow horse made of wood. The Trojans brought the horse inside the town walls, and the

Greeks came out of it that night and set fire to everything. They killed the men of Troy, and made slaves of the women and children."

"That's right," I said. "But the Greeks didn't kill all the Trojans. Some of them escaped. For seven years they have been looking for a new homeland. And now they have come here. King Latinus wants to give them land and his daughter Lavinia. But Queen Amata thinks they are pirates. She wants Lavinia to marry her nephew Turnus."

"Is Lavinia here today?" Camilla asked.

I nodded. "See that tall girl at the very front?" I pointed. "Behind the bull?"

We had come to the Hill of Pluto and we could see the whole line of girls before us. Camilla looked at the girl I was pointing out. She had golden hair, milky skin and a slender waist. She walked beside Tulla, but she outshone her as the sun outshines the moon.

"She's beautiful," Camilla breathed. "And who is Turnus?"

"He is the prince of a town near by," I said. "He is young and handsome. They say the Trojan Leader is old and barbaric."

"Poor Lavinia," Camilla whispered. "I belong to Diana, so I will never wed."

We had to be silent then, for we had reached the altar. We all stood around it in a curved line, our heads bowed.

In a loud voice, the priest prayed to Pluto and asked him to accept the offering. As he prayed, his two helpers moved closer to the bull.

Camilla tugged the sleeve of my tunic. "Don't they give the bull special grain to make him sleepy?" she whispered.

I nodded. "Of course."

Her grubby face creased in a frown. "That bull doesn't look sleepy."

Camilla was right. The bull looked nervous.

As one helper pushed his head down, the other prepared to stun the animal with an axe-blow to the base of its skull. But just as he swung, the bull moved. The blade fell on the bull's side, and he rose with a bellow as blood spurted out. Girls screamed as the wounded bull shook off the man holding his horns. Then the bull turned and charged straight at us.

6

THE BEAST

The bull charged the circle of screaming girls. It was mad with pain.

The helper's mouth hung open as Camilla darted forward and grabbed his axe.

As the bull thundered past, she swung it.

Her aim was true. She struck the bull at the base of his skull.

He dropped like a huge rock at her feet.

But the bull was only stunned. The priest rushed forward and cut its throat, catching the gush of blood in his silver bucket.

Now the bull was dead and the sacrifice completed.

Everyone turned to Camilla and cheered.

The priest and his two helpers stretched out their hands to her and bowed.

The little girls rushed forward to hug her. The older girls patted her back with shy hands.

The priest raised his hands. "A bad omen has been turned into a good one!" His voice was so loud that the people on the town wall could hear. He gestured towards Camilla. "A maiden has sent the gift down to the Underworld." He turned to the rest of us. "Come!" he said, as his helpers began to skin the bull. "Let us dance the dance of new life!"

All the girls held out eager hands to Camilla, even Larina, Tulla and Tarpi.

But she turned to me. "Acca," she said.

Full of joy, I took her hand. We danced and laughed to welcome the Girl Goddess back to the Upperworld.

Later, Camilla and I spread her cloak of bear skin on the grass. We sat on it and ate roast meat from the bull. Camilla hunched over her food and ate like an animal. I saw that her fingernails were black with grime. When she finished eating, she wiped her mouth on the back of her hand and burped.

The priests' helpers were passing out dried figs and almonds, and I noticed that more people had gathered on the town walls. Not just the proud parents of the girls, but everybody – merchants, priests, even old King Latinus and Queen Amata. When they saw Camilla glance towards them, they cheered.

Camilla looked at me. Her mouth was greasy from the meat and her cheeks bulged with figs. "Are they cheering for me?" she asked.

"Yes," I said. "You're famous. They love that you killed the bull before it hurt anyone."

She swallowed her food, then looked back at the town wall.

"Have you ever killed such a big animal before?" I asked.

She took another handful of figs and almonds. "Of course. I could throw a javelin almost before I could walk," she said. "I killed a crane with my sling when I was five. I have killed bears, wolves, wild boar and once a panther. I can use a spear and an axe. Plus bow and arrows, of course."

I had a sudden impulse.

"Camilla," I said. "Come live with me and my mother."

"Live with you … in the town?" she said. "But I've never even been inside a town before. I belong to Diana, goddess of the woods. A cave is my bedroom and bear skin my bed. My hearth is a campfire and my bath is the brook. I wouldn't know how to live in a town. I would miss the stars. Also," she looked at the other girls, "they mocked me."

"They're not mocking you any more," I said. "You won their hearts. And don't worry." I took her grimy hands in mine. "We don't have to spend lots of time in the town. We can spend our days outside in the woods and use my house just to sleep in. There is a little yard with an open roof. We can make a bed for you there so you can see the stars."

For a moment she looked at me. Then she shook her head.

"I'm sorry, Acca. I can't."

Before I could protest, she stood up and ran down the hill towards the woods. Almo was right – she ran faster than any person I have ever seen. But with her rusty tunic flapping around her and the cow horns in her hair, she looked like some strange wild creature.

From the town walls came laughter and cheers. Or were they jeers?

I turned to look at the three rich girls, but they were not laughing.

"Make her come back!" Tulla cried, and the others nodded.

I turned to watch Camilla. From Pluto's Hill I could see the point at which she entered the woods, and rising birds showed me her path.

She was fleeing to her cave, and I was almost certain I knew where it was.

I turned to the girls. "I will bring her back," I said. "But when I do, you must help me."

7

CAMILLA'S CAVE

The next day I rose before dawn and dressed in my hunting clothes. I folded my new leaf-green silk tunic and slipped it down the front of my old moss-green one, along with a yellow cord. I hung a skin of water over one arm and a quiver over the other. I took my bow in my right hand.

I was first out the town gates when the guards opened them at dawn.

They were used to seeing me go out early to hunt, but that morning they frowned at me.

"Are you not afraid of Trojans?" one of them said. "Queen Amata says their spies are everywhere. She told us to keep a sharp lookout."

"I won't go far," I lied. "I just want to catch some nice game for my mother's birthday."

But before I entered the woods, I took a deep breath and asked Diana to protect me. And to help me find Camilla.

I ran deep into the cool woods and made for the mountains to the south-east.

A scuffed path took me deeper.

Sweet birdsong filled the air.

The sun rose higher, and sent golden spears of light into the glade.

For a moment, I seemed to hear the sounds of women dancing in a grove sacred to the God of Wine, but I passed them by. I had seen the print of Camilla's bare foot in the dust between the oak trees.

Later, I thought I heard men's voices speaking in a strange accent. But I had found the hoof prints of a horse Camilla had mounted, so I did not turn aside.

It was the sound of splashing water that led me to her. I pushed past fragrant shrubs, and emerged into a bright clearing with a golden cliff face. A slender waterfall tumbled down its face and near by was a dark hole – the mouth of a cave.

I went past a much-used campfire and looked into the cave. Its roof was black with smoke. On the earth floor were two fur beds. Weapons leaned against the curving stone walls. I saw spears, axes, javelins. Also two bows and two quivers full of arrows.

"How did you find my home?" Camilla's voice came from behind me.

I turned and smiled.

She had been weeping again.

"The goddess Diana led me here." I stepped forward and took her hands. "Aren't you lonely? Don't you want to be with other people?"

She hung her head and nodded. "I long for friends. But my father made a vow for me. I am dedicated to Diana."

"Maybe you could be her priestess, but live in the town," I said. "You could help other girls become her followers."

Her eyes lit up, then grew dark again. "But the other girls mocked me," she said. "They think I'm strange."

"You weren't what they expected," I told her. "But after you saved us from the bull, they begged me to bring you back."

"They did?"

"Yes! Come back to Laurentum with me. We'll show you how to live among people and you can teach us to worship Diana. Here." I reached into the neck of my old moss-green tunic and took out the new silk one. "A gift for you."

"Really?"

"Really." I turned away, in case she was too shy to undress before me. When I turned back she had put it on.

"Now belt it like this." I handed her the yellow cord. "Put it around your waist and make an X across your chest, so it shows your shape." I stood back. "Beautiful."

She blushed and stroked the silk. "It feels wonderful."

And, for the first time, I saw her show her teeth in a smile.

"Oh!" I winced. "Your teeth. Do you ever brush them?"

"I use a tooth stick sometimes," she said.

I stepped closer. "Open up. Let me see. None of them are rotten. A little tooth powder will bring out the white again. Do you have a mirror?"

"Mirror?" She frowned.

"A shiny silver disc. You can see yourself in it."

She tilted her head to one side – she still didn't understand.

"You know how sometimes you can see your face in a still pond?" I said. "A mirror is like that. Only much clearer, and you can hold it up."

Her eyes grew wide. "Do you have a mirror at your home?"

"Of course! And tooth powder to make your teeth white as pearls."

"Pearls?" she said.

I laughed. "You have a lot to learn."

She smiled back, then covered her mouth. "Is there somewhere for Puerina to stay?"

"Who's Puerina?"

"My horse. She was wild, but Father helped me tame her. I will call her." She whistled like a bird.

"Before we were poor," I said, "we used to have a donkey. There is still a stall in our house. Your horse can sleep there."

A moment later the bushes parted and a lovely white horse stepped into the glade.

Camilla hugged Puerina's neck and hid her face in the white mane for a long moment. Then she turned to me and nodded. "If you show me how to be live among people and look beautiful, I will show you how to worship Diana, goddess of the hunt."

8

INTO THE TOWN

Camilla's pretty white mare carried us swiftly out of the woods. We rode bareback, with Camilla in front. I sat with my arms around Camilla's slender waist. I could feel her body – firm and warm – through the thin silk of the leaf-green tunic.

I had found the girl of my childhood dreams. I had never been so happy.

It was dusk when we reached the gates of Laurentum. Camilla made the horse stop and tipped her head to gaze up at the high stone walls.

"Are there trees inside the town?" she asked in a small voice.

"Of course!" I said. "The royal palace is surrounded by an ancient grove. Have you really never been in a town before?"

She shook her head.

"Don't worry," I said. "You will soon get used to it."

So Camilla patted Puerina's neck, took a deep breath and clucked with her tongue.

The guards gave us a nod and one of them leaned forward on his spear to peer at Camilla. Then he settled back against the wall with a shrug.

We rode to my house and Camilla met my mother.

We put Puerina in the stall that had once belonged to our donkey. We gave her a meal of oat mash and I forked out an old bale of hay for the floor.

Then we walked up the smooth stony streets to Larina's house.

Larina lived on the slopes by the palace. Her house had four servants, three inner gardens and its own bath houses.

Larina greeted us both with a warm smile. I had shared my plan with the three rich girls the day before.

"Step into the house with your right foot," I whispered to Camilla. "Or it's bad luck."

Camilla obeyed, gazing about in wonder. The walls were green, red and blue, with borders of white birds on black. The ceilings had coloured patterns on them too, and even the pillars were painted. Larina looked Camilla up and down with a practised eye. She was the most fashionable girl in Laurentum, next to Princess Lavinia.

"My mother spent the day with the Queen," Larina said. "They were doing something in the woods, but she won't say what. She just got back and went to bed with no supper. Tulla and Tarpi will be here soon. The bath is heating. First, come have something to eat."

When she walked or rode, Camilla held herself like a Queen. But when she ate, she bent over her food like a wild animal. We showed her how to lie on her left side and take dainty morsels with her right hand. We made her chew each bite ten times with her mouth closed. We told her not to burp afterwards, but to sip a little watered wine.

She obeyed, happy to taste food she had never tried before. All her life she'd drunk water or milk. Her only food had been game and woodland fruits. Venison with berries. Rabbit and wild garlic. Bear and pine-nut stew.

She had never tried bread. Never tasted an olive! And the cheese she and her father made was watery, not firm.

When the other two girls arrived, the five of us crossed a garden to the bath house. Camilla stopped and looked up.

"I like it that this house has sky with stars," she said.

The others stopped and looked up, too.

"I never thought of that," Tarpi said.

There were two rooms in Larina's bath house, and a round hot bath deep enough for us all to stand in with the steaming water up to our necks. I was impressed, for I had only been to the public bath house. But Camilla was thrilled. She had never bathed in warm water that smelled of roses, only cold streams and chilly brooks.

Her joy made it seem new to us, too. We soaked and splashed and laughed. Then we pinched our noses and ducked our heads under to soak our hair. After a while, we came out and sat on benches to cool our steaming bodies.

I showed Camilla how to clean herself by rubbing oil on her body and then scraping it off with a blunt bronze blade.

Tulla used a wooden comb to brush the tangles from Camilla's light brown locks.

Tarpi rubbed the little hairs off her legs with a piece of pumice.

Larina showed Camilla how to clean her teeth with charcoal powder. At first it made her teeth even blacker, but when she rinsed her mouth with a beaker of vinegar and water they came up almost white.

After another dip in the steamy hot pool, we went back to the warm changing room where the air was clear and the pine torches burned bright.

I helped Camilla rub scented oil on her body to keep the skin soft.

Tulla pinned Camilla's hair up in curls with bits of cloth.

Tarpi shaped her nails with a bronze file.

Larina showed Camilla how to outline her eyes with black kohl and stain her lips with red wine dregs.

Then we dressed her in my leaf-green silk tunic, a pink velvet cloak of Larina's and a pair of golden sandals that were too small for Tarpi. Tulla unpinned Camilla's hair. It was almost dry, and it fell down her back in a mass of curls. I saw that its true colour was not brown, but the deep gold of a lion skin.

We stood back and clapped, for Camilla looked as lovely as any princess.

Larina got her big silver mirror and we held it for Camilla to see herself.

"Is that me?" Camilla asked. She leaned closer. "My eyes *are* green!" She smiled. "And look! My teeth are white! I'm beautiful!"

We laughed at her innocent joy.

Then she kissed each of us in turn.

We were still laughing and chattering when a female servant opened the door. "There is a messenger here," she said. "Queen Amata wants to see Princess Camilla."

The room fell silent.

Larina cocked her head and narrowed her eyes. "Now?" she said. "In the middle of the night?"

"Yes," the servant replied. Her face was pale. "The Queen's messenger said you must come right now."

9

THE JEALOUS QUEEN

"How does the Queen know Camilla is here?" Larina asked me when the servant had gone. "Did anyone see you enter the city?"

"I don't know," I said. "The guards didn't recognise her."

Tarpi hung her frizzy head. "I might have said something to my father," she admitted.

"Why does it matter?" Tulla asked.

Larina lowered her voice. "Everyone knows that Queen Amata is desperate for Turnus to marry her daughter. What if he wants to marry Camilla instead?"

"But Camilla is devoted to Diana and has vowed never to marry," I protested.

"Look at her," Larina said. "Does she look like she will never wed?"

We all looked at Camilla. Her mane of dark gold curls. Her black-lined green eyes. Her full red lips. Her beautiful body. She was stunning.

"Do you think Queen Amata will want her future son-in-law to meet such a beautiful warrior?" Larina went on. "One who is a princess?"

"Larina's right," Tulla said. "We can't let the Queen see how beautiful Camilla is!"

So we made poor Camilla put on her grubby man's tunic and swish her mouth with charcoal water to make her teeth look grey again.

Outside, in the light of torches, we rubbed dust into her hair to make it drab and pulled it back to hide the bouncy curls. We streaked her face with dirt and rubbed off the red lip tint.

Larina found an old pair of her younger brother's boots and we put them on Camilla's feet to make her seem more like a boy.

"There!" Larina cried. "Now she can see the Queen."

"Go with her, Acca," Tarpi said to me. "Tell her Camilla is staying with you."

The messenger's torch lit our way up the night streets of the town to the palace in its dark and sacred grove. Camilla clutched my hand.

It must have been nearly midnight by the time we were shown into the Queen's part of the palace.

The big room was lit by two dozen lamps, and it glittered like a box of jewels. The marble columns were pink and green. The mosaic floor sparkled with gold. All the couches were covered with silk tapestries.

Camilla stared with her mouth open, and I saw Queen Amata smirk as she moved forward.

"Princess Camilla," she said. "Welcome to Laurentum."

Queen Amata was much younger than her husband the King, and very beautiful. Only her mouth spoiled the effect, for her lips were thin.

Camilla grasped the Queen's hand, as one man grasps the hand of another. The Queen looked amused rather than angry, and she turned to me. "You are her servant?" she asked.

"A friend, oh Queen." I bowed.

Camilla clumped over in her heavy boots to examine a painting on a wall. "Look!" she cried. "It's the Greeks coming out of the horse's belly!"

"Such a shame they didn't kill all the Trojans," Queen Amata murmured. She played with her gold snake necklace. "Please sit."

Camilla plonked herself down on the nearest couch.

"Would you like some refreshments?" the Queen asked. She sat with grace on the nearest couch. I sat next to Camilla.

Camilla crinkled her grubby nose. "Some what?"

Queen Amata smiled. "Refreshments."

"She means food," I whispered in Camilla's ear.

"Gods, yes!" Camilla cried. "I could eat a wild boar!"

Once again the Queen smirked. At first I was angry, but then I reminded myself that the Queen would never see this Camilla as a threat.

A servant girl brought a tray heavy with almonds, dates and a wedge of the finest goat cheese. There was a small knife for the cheese. It had a handle made of mother-of-pearl.

Camilla looked at me.

"Eat like you normally do," I said out of the corner of my mouth, "not the way we showed you this evening."

Now it was Queen Amata's turn to stare with her mouth open, for Camilla fell upon the "refreshments" like a wolf upon a lamb. She picked up the wedge of cheese and ate it in six big bites. Then she tossed down handfuls of almonds and crunched them with her mouth open so that bits of nut flew out. Last, she held up a date and looked at it from all angles. Then she sniffed it. As soon as she tasted it, she threw back her head and howled in joy before gobbling up every one.

The Queen laughed and I have to confess that I did, too.

Wine came next, warm and spiced and sweet with honey. And strong.

"Go easy," I whispered to Camilla. "It's almost neat!"

But she drained her goblet in great gulps and came up gasping.

All of a sudden she froze, like a cat when it has seen a mouse. Then, fast as a whip crack, she darted towards one of the columns, pulled a girl out from behind it and held the little cheese knife to her throat.

The Queen screamed.

I gasped.

"Spy!" Camilla bellowed. "Assassin!"

"No!" Queen Amata jumped to her feet and held up both hands. "It's Princess Lavinia! My daughter."

Camilla was holding the princess from behind so I could see both their faces, side by side.

Lavinia's big blue eyes were rolling with terror.

Camilla's dust-streaked face, grey teeth and pulled-back hair made her look like a barbarian. Her man's tunic and heavy boots increased this impression.

"Please," Queen Amata cried. "Don't hurt her. Lavinia wasn't spying. She's just shy."

With a grunt of disgust, Camilla pushed Lavinia forward. The girl fell sobbing into her mother's arms.

"Princess Camilla," the Queen said, her voice now icy. "Why have you come to Laurentum?"

Camilla stood with her feet planted apart and her fists on her hips. "I want to honour Diana by bringing her other virgin hunters," she said. "I came here to train four girls from this town to be followers of the goddess."

Queen Amata helped Lavinia sit down. Then she walked to the painting of the Trojan horse.

Her back was to us as she spoke. "My husband the King is old and foolish," she said. "He does not realise that the Trojans are a band of pirates. He does not realise that my nephew Turnus is meant for Lavinia." She turned and looked at Camilla. "Would you be willing to fight, if needs be? To protect your friends here in Laurentum?"

"Yes," Camilla said. "My father showed me how to fight as well as hunt. He said I was born for battle."

"And would you be willing to train followers of Diana who can fight as well as hunt?"

Camilla looked at me. My heart was pounding but I gave her a nod in reply.

"Yes!" said Camilla.

"Excellent!" The Queen clapped her hands. "A band of Amazons would put those pretty-boy Trojans in their place. And it would encourage our own troops. Tell me what you need, and I will provide it."

Camilla stroked her chin as a man might stroke his beard. I realised it was something her father must have done.

"We need weapons," she said. "And armour." She put her fists back on her hips and nodded. "That will be a good start."

"Very well." The Queen was trying not to smile. "Come back tomorrow morning and I will give you all you ask for."

The Queen led her trembling daughter over to an inner door, then she looked back at Camilla. "Welcome to Laurentum, Princess Camilla."

10

THE HUNTER'S ARROW

The next morning the five of us collected axes, swords and javelins from the palace.

We giggled as we tried on bronze breast-plates. None of them fit and so the armourer said he would make us some of our own.

Back in the yard of my house, Camilla showed us how to use a sword. She helped us improve our aim with a bow. She showed us how to swing an axe with the double blade and how to use a shield as a weapon, by bringing it up under a man's chin.

We laughed as we trained and we panted with the joy of it.

My mother stood at the door and shook her head.

But after a while she went into the house to prepare us a lunch of garlic cheese, black olives and dates as sweet as honey.

While we ate, Camilla told us something her father had once said.

"You must be Cyclops for the hunt, but Argus in a battle."

Tulla frowned. "What does that mean?"

"The Cyclops has only one eye," Camilla said. "And Argus had one hundred eyes all over his body."

"We all know that," Tarpi said. "But what does it mean?"

I was puzzled, too. "Don't you chase a man in a battle, just as you chase a deer in the hunt?"

Camilla put down her plate and picked up a battle-axe. "Yes, but for the hunt all your focus is on the animal you are following."

Tarpi's face lit up. "Like the single eye of the Cyclops," she said.

"Yes." Camilla threw the axe at the stable door. She had drawn the outline of a warrior on it with a big piece of charcoal. Her axe struck the man's helmet. "But for the battle," she said, "you need to have eyes all over your body."

"Like Argus!" Tulla cried.

"Exactly!" Camilla walked to the stable door and pulled the axe from the wood. "In a battle you need Argus's eyes because danger can come from any side."

"In a battle you are both the hunter and the hunted," Tarpi cried.

"Yes." Camilla walked back towards us. "You might be aiming for someone over there." She pointed at the double front doors leading into our courtyard. "When danger comes upon you from behind!" She whirled and threw her axe. It struck the charcoal man again, this time in his chest.

Her advice made me shiver.

I loved hunting because of the woods and the dappled sunshine and the peace. But it always made me sad to kill an animal and watch the life fade from its eyes. I wondered how it would be to kill a man.

At that moment we heard a girl outside call my name.

"It's Silvia," I said, and I ran to the double doors.

When I opened them, Silvia fell into my arms.

"They shot him!" she cried. "An arrow in the gut. He came home last night. He was groaning in pain."

"Your pet stag?" I cried.

"Yes," she sobbed. She looked at me with swollen eyes. "Acca, it took him all night to die!"

I heard the brassy blare of a war trumpet somewhere outside the town walls.

A slow anger started to fill me.

"Who did this?" I cried.

"A hunting party of Trojans," she said. "They say it was the leader's son who shot him."

Camilla stepped forward, and her green eyes blazed.

"The deer with the garland is yours?" she said. "I have seen it many times. Any fool can tell it is a pet!"

"Queen Amata was right," Tarpi cried. "The Trojans are barbarians!"

"That's not all!" Silvia cried. "Some shepherds and herdsmen have gone to take revenge on the hunters." She gripped my hands. "Acca, my father went with them. And my brothers, too!"

"Come on!" Camilla said. She put on her quiver full of arrows and took her bow and three javelins.

We all grabbed our weapons and ran out of the house.

When we reached the town gates we were just in time to see them bring back the bodies on stretchers made of woven branches.

The first was a white-haired old man who used to sit at the town gates. He had been kind and gentle with a twinkle in his eye. He was always the first to step between angry men and bring peace. His face was a mass of blood, smashed with something sharp.

There were other bodies. Shepherds and herdsmen. They had fought with shepherd's staffs and wooden clubs, but the Trojans had used spears of iron and bronze swords.

Silvia's father took up the end of the procession. He was weeping and tugging his hair. I ran forward to see the last dead body.

It was my friend Almo, Silvia's brother. Only fourteen. His skin was as white as a lily and blood blossomed around an arrow in his throat.

Silvia screamed and fell at our feet in a faint.

I felt rage chill my bones. Like cold fire.

A few moments before, I had wondered how I would ever be able to kill a man. Now I knew that if that man was a Trojan, I would have no problem.

11

AMAZONS OF LAURENTUM

Now that we knew the true nature of the Trojans, we began to train in earnest.

Camilla had shown us how to use weapons on foot, but we also needed to learn how to fight on horseback. I had no horse and the three girls only had ponies, so we went to the royal stables.

The keeper gave me a black mare called Placida.

The other girls claimed three chestnut mares. They had been part of a chariot team and they were happy to be in action together again.

Early the next morning we rode out into the field by the town walls where the young men had played their War Games. The three rich girls and I wore leaf-green tunics with long sleeves to match Camilla's. My mother and Tulla's aunt had made us green leggings for modesty. We were the Amazons of Laurentum. We wore our hair loose. It felt wonderful.

When we rode out with our bows and arrows slung across our bodies and our light javelins, the men on the plain gave a great cheer.

Some of them called out rude things, but they were smiling.

Camilla's eyes blazed with anger, but I soothed her. "Don't take any notice," I said. "It is a strange mark of respect."

Then one man shouted louder than the rest.

"Hey, Princess Curly Top!" he called to Camilla. "Let me put my sword in your scabbard!" I saw her cheeks flush pink but she turned round on her horse so that she was riding backwards. Then she pulled out her bronze axe and swung it around her head. "Only if you let me store my axe in your chest!" she yelled back.

"Whoa!" the man cried. "Maybe another time then!"

Everybody laughed and we heard a spatter of cheers from above. The people of Laurentum had flocked to the city walls to watch us.

At the foot of the wall, workers had been digging a ditch. Now they were staring at us with open mouths.

When Camilla saw what they were doing, she frowned. "Aren't your town walls strong enough?" she asked.

Tulla shrugged. "Perhaps. But my father says the Trojans believe it is their destiny to have this land. And they have nothing to lose. It is better for us to be safe than sorry."

Camilla gave a grim nod. "Then let us give them hope with our bravery!" she said.

Over the next few hours, she showed us how to throw our javelins from our horses' backs.

She showed us how to swing a sword or battle-axe. "Don't go for the man unless he is an easy target," she said. "Go for his horse. If it rears and comes down on top of him you will have stopped them both."

Last, she showed us how to turn and fire arrows behind us. This was what we would do if we had to retreat. This task looked difficult but it proved easy once we got up the courage to try it.

I looked up and saw envy on the faces of the other girls on the wall.

At one point the five of us were riding backwards in a row. As our arrows peppered the field behind us, I felt a surge of joy and I seemed to float above myself. I could almost see us down below – five gold-green Amazons with our lion-haired leader in the middle.

At that moment I realised that my love for Camilla was a gift from the gods. I prayed. "Thank you Diana, Minerva and Juno, or whichever of you gods put this fire in my heart. I know why I am alive. I exist for Camilla."

As we came near the new ditch in front of the town walls, Camilla gave a low command. We swivelled back round on our horses so that we faced forward. On Camilla's second command we made our horses stop.

Cheers from the wall above poured down on us like late summer rain on thirsty earth.

Then Tulla gasped. The rest of us turned to see a man riding towards us on a white horse with black splashes. We could not see his face, for he wore a bronze helmet with three red feathers.

"Who is he?" Camilla asked.

"Turnus," I said. "The great hero."

"And the man who should marry Princess Lavinia," Larina added.

Tulla gave a deep sigh. "Every woman in Laurentum loves him."

Camilla lifted her chin. "Not me."

As Turnus came closer, he took off his helmet, so we could see his handsome face and his glossy mane of black hair.

His bronze shin-guards seemed to be pure gold. His breast-plate had scales like a fish, made of yellow brass. In the morning sun, he was almost too dazzling to look upon.

"Oh," Camilla gasped. Her hands went to her flushed cheeks.

I saw Larina and Tarpi look at one another and then grin.

I felt a stab of jealousy.

"Now do you love him?" Tarpi said with a wink.

"No," Camilla said. "I love his armour."

12

THE GREAT WARRIORS MEET

Turnus swung off his horse and landed on the ground with a golden clang.

Camilla gave a low command. The five of us swung our right legs up and over our horses' necks and slid down their left sides.

Turnus put his helmet on the ground and came towards us.

"Princess Camilla?" he said.

Camilla stepped forward and put out her hand with the palm down as we had showed her. Turnus bent and kissed her fingers.

She told him each of our names and he kissed our fingers, too. Up close, he was magnificent, with smooth skin and black eyes and white teeth. Poor Tulla almost fainted with love. Larina's cheeks were bright pink.

Camilla's cheeks were pink, too, but her eyes were on the brass scales of his armour and his golden weapons.

"Amazons," Turnus said. "Thank you for joining us. I salute you!" Then in a lower voice he said, "I have a favour to ask of you."

Camilla smiled, and her teeth were white as pearls. "Name it, my lord."

"You are the Queen of Privernum, correct?"

"Yes." Camilla's smile wobbled. "I suppose I am. My father was King of Privernum, and now he has died."

Turnus nodded. "The Trojans have shown us their true nature," he said. "They killed harmless shepherds and herdsmen, old men and boys. I have asked all of our allies to send troops to help us. My own town of Ardea is sending one thousand men. Can you help?"

Camilla waved at us. "We are yours to command."

"Yes," Turnus said. "You five girls are inspiring. But I need far more. Could you go back to your home town of Privernum and bring back a troop of your cavalry? It could win us the war."

Camilla's face was as pale as ivory. For a moment I thought she was going to faint.

Then she did something that surprised us all. She jumped onto Puerina, dug in her heels and galloped off into the woods.

Turnus looked after her with a frown.

"That's not the way to Privernum," he said. Then he turned to me. "Is she afraid?"

I swung up onto Placida's back. "Camilla is the bravest person I have ever met," I said. "I don't know where she's going but I promise you will have your troops. Come on, Amazons!" I cried to my friends. "Let's follow Camilla."

13

FAITHFUL FOLLOWERS

I had no idea why Camilla fled from Turnus, but I knew where she would go.

When we reached Camilla's cave, we saw her horse in the clearing, white against the golden cliff and its waterfall. She was loosely tied to a blue pine. The four of us came down off our own horses and tied them near Puerina.

"Will you wait here for a moment?" I asked the others.

They nodded and Tarpi stepped forward. "Tell her she is our leader," she said. "We will go where she goes."

I went to the cave and peered in. Camilla sat huddled in a corner, weeping.

I sat beside her.

She turned and hid her face in my hair. Now the sobs came louder. I held her and stroked her and let her cry.

At last her tears stopped. She dried her cheeks on the green silk sleeve of her tunic.

"Are the others with you?" she said.

I nodded. "We are devoted to you."

"Tell them to come in."

"Girls!" I called. "You can come."

My arm was still around her slender form as she told us why she had run away.

"You know the story of how I came to grow up here?" she asked.

Larina nodded. "The baby on the spear," she said. "We all heard it when we were children."

"Did they ever tell you what my father was running from?" she asked.

I shook my head. So did Larina and Tulla, but Tarpi looked at the ground, then nodded. "My father is on the council," she said. "He knows about politics." She looked at Camilla. "He said your father was cruel to his people. His own subjects wanted to kill him."

"Yes," Camilla said softly. "My father was a harsh ruler. He taxed his people so he could be rich. But see what good it did him." She looked around the cave. "They drove him out and he spent the last fifteen years of his life here, wearing animal skins and eating roast squirrel and drinking sour milk."

My arm was still around her and I could feel her whole body shake.

"They didn't just want to kill him," she said. "They wanted to kill me, too." She looked at us, and her green eyes were rimmed with red. "Why do you think I came to Laurentum instead of Privernum, my own home town?"

I took her hands in mine. "Camilla," I said. "You are not your father. Your people might welcome you. Think of how much our people love you."

"Your people only love me when I wear beautiful clothes and ride backwards on a horse." Camilla looked at each of us in turn. "And they love it when the four of you ride with me."

Tarpi stood up. "Then we will come to your home town with you!"

Camilla's brows went up. "What if they kill you along with me?"

"We are prepared to die with you," Tulla said.

Larina rose to her feet with grace. "We are your servants."

I stood up, too. "We will do whatever you ask."

"Except bare one breast," Tulla said with a giggle.

We all laughed but then we wasted no more time. We mounted our horses and rode south.

For the first time in sixteen years, Camilla was going home.

14

CAMILLA GOES HOME

At dusk we came to a shallow river. On our side was an ancient forest of cedar, rowan and ash. On the far bank were olive trees and cork oaks. We came down off our horses and drank. The water was as clear as glass.

Camilla stood up and wiped her mouth with the back of her arm. "There it is," she said. "The town where I was born. Privernum."

The four of us followed her gaze.

On a hill to the south was a town of square houses with flat roofs the same colour as the rocks around.

"Is this the famous river?" I asked. "The one you flew over on a spear?"

"Yes." Camilla laughed at the look on my face. "This is it."

"Do you remember it?" I asked. "When your father threw you across the river?"

Our horses lifted their dripping muzzles from the river and turned, as if they wanted to hear the answer, too.

Camilla shook her head. "No. But sometimes I dream I am flying."

We went without dinner that evening, but the night was mild and the sky full of stars. We slept on our cloaks, and huddled together for warmth with our horses hobbled around us. Sometime in the night I woke and went into the bushes. When I came back, I saw Camilla's eyes gleam in the moonlight. "Are you awake?" I whispered.

"Yes," she said. "I'm chilly. Come and warm me up."

As we lay in one another's arms and gazed up at the night sky, I remembered how my father had pointed out the different star groups. Pegasus the Flying Horse. The Throne of Juno. We had even made up one for Baby Camilla on Her Spear.

The thought of my father made my eyes fill with tears.

I felt her head turn to look at me. "Are you sad?" Camilla whispered.

"No, I'm happy," I told her. "I was just thinking of my father."

"Is he the reason you want to fight?"

In my mind, I saw my father giving me my toy bow and arrows on my 5th birthday. "No," I said. "You're the reason."

"Me?"

"Yes," I said. "My father used to tell me about you. When I was almost five, he saw you in your tiger skin. From that moment on, I wanted to be like you."

"And I longed to be like you," Camilla said. "I used to watch you girls in the spring Festival and hear you giggle and talk about boys and marriage."

"Do you want to marry?" I asked.

"I don't know," she whispered. "But at least you have a choice. The moment I flew over this river I belonged to Diana. My life was hers."

Camilla paused and then turned her head to look up at the stars. "And if I am a Queen then my life belongs to my people."

I looked up, too. I searched for Baby Camilla on Her Spear, but I could not find that star group. Instead I found five bright stars in a cluster above us.

"Diana, please preserve us in the days to come," I prayed under my breath.

But as I watched, the biggest of the five stars fell from the sky and vanished.

15

THE SPEECH BY THE RIVER

The next morning we woke at dawn, stiff and hungry.

A long drink of cold river water helped our hunger a little. We walked and became less stiff.

"Before we go up to the town," Camilla said, "I want to practise my speech. Tell me if it is good or not."

The four of us sat on our cloaks and looked at her. The rising sun at her back made her hair look like a dark gold flame around her head.

"People of Privernum," she began in her clear voice. "Twenty years ago your King married a beautiful woman. He loved her deeply and they lived happily for over three years. But she died giving birth to a little girl. The King was mad with grief, and he took out his anger on you. He taxed you. He stole your fields, crops and animals. He made you work long hours. You could not endure his cruelty. When his baby girl was only five months old, you drove him out."

Camilla placed her right hand on her chest and bowed her head.

"I am that girl. I am Camilla." She lifted her head. "I have returned to beg your forgiveness and to serve you. If you believe that I am worthy, give me a band of cavalry and I will lead them against the Trojans. I do not claim the title of Queen. I only claim the title of Your Servant."

The four of us jumped to our feet and clapped and cheered.

"How can the people of Privernum refuse you?" I cried. "They will grant all your requests."

And I was right.

When we reached Privernum, 200 horsemen rode out to meet us. They came down and kneeled in the dust before her. The people welcomed us with open gates and open arms. Their leader was old and fearful, and his younger subjects longed to join the fight against the Trojans.

On the first day they feasted us and Camilla met all the important people in the town.

On the second day they gave Camilla a golden bow and silver arrows.

On the third day we left for Laurentum.

The elders of Privernum had promised that if Camilla returned as the victor, they would make her their Queen.

16

WAITING TO ATTACK NEW TROY

Travelling with 200 men on horseback is slow. After a long day's ride we reached Ardea, the home town of Turnus. It was getting dark, so we set up camp outside the town walls.

Soon a line of torches showed us that the people were coming to meet us, with hot food for hungry horsemen. Turnus's sister Juturna led them to us. She had flashing dark eyes and a mane of black hair, and she was as beautiful as Turnus was handsome. She invited Camilla and the four of us to spend the night in her palace.

We were happy to accept. We fell into deep sleep on a giant bed, our legs and arms entwined.

The next morning Juturna brought us a feast for breakfast.

We had been too tired to eat the night before and we fell on it like wolves.

"Stop, Amazons!" Camilla cried.

We all froze in the act of chewing.

"Dainty bites," Camilla said. "And chew each mouthful ten times."

We all laughed, but I saw how far Camilla had come.

After breakfast, Juturna took us to her private bath house. We splashed together in a pool that sparkled with tiny gold and glass tiles. It was like the first night at Larina's house, only better. We were now devoted to one another.

It was noon by the time we were dressed and dry. The troops outside had been ready for hours. We could hear them chanting for Camilla.

When we rode out of the city gates, their cheers reached the heavens.

Camilla looked magnificent. Juturna had given her a filmy white tunic and a short purple cape. She wore her golden bow and her silver arrows in a painted quiver.

Her cheeks were tinted pink with the natural blush of excitement.

As we neared Laurentum, a lone horseman galloped out to meet us.

"Queen Camilla!" he cried. "A message from Turnus! He says the Trojan leader has gone north to get help from our enemies, the Arcadians and the Etruscans. He left most of his men in a wooden fort, under the command of his son. Turnus says if we attack the fort now, we can destroy them! He begs you to join him with all the forces you have."

And so we passed my home town of Laurentum without stopping, and rode on north to help Turnus.

When we arrived at the river Tiber, the sun was low in the sky.

The ground was covered with so many of our troops that we could only see the enemy fort from a distance. Three of its walls were made of split pine logs. The last wall was the river itself – wide and deep and tawny.

"What's happening?" Camilla said. "Everyone is in ranks but nobody is fighting."

"I think I see Turnus!" Tulla stood on her horse's back to get the best view. "He's there, in front of the fort."

She pointed and we saw Turnus on his black and white horse, with the red feathers in his helmet and his dazzling armour.

We could hear him shouting, but not the words.

"What is he doing?" Camilla asked the captain of a troop of cavalry.

"He's daring them to come out and fight," the captain replied. "Says he'll burn the fort down if they don't."

We could all see the heads of the Trojans looking down from the wooden walls of the fort. They stared at Turnus in silence and made no move to open the gates.

"They call that wooden fort New Troy," Tarpi said.

"Why doesn't he just put a torch to it and burn it down?" Larina asked.

"He wants to fight," Camilla said. "He wants the glory."

"Fool!" Tarpi muttered. "He should just burn them alive."

The thought of burning men alive made me shudder. Then I saw something.

"Look!" I cried. "He's setting fire to their ships!"

"Good!" Camilla punched her fist in the air. "Now they will have no way to leave."

"Don't we want them to leave?" I said. "Wouldn't it be better if they just went far away and left us alone?"

"No!" Camilla cried. "Have you forgotten what those barbarians did to Silvia's deer?"

"They killed her brother!" Larina said.

"And the shepherds," Tarpi said.

It was almost dark when a messenger from Turnus galloped up. The armies would attack in the morning. Turnus would send word to each commander to tell them when it was time to join the battle.

The next morning we heard that two young Trojans had crept into the camp in the night, in order to warn their absent leader of the siege. But they made a fatal mistake. As they stopped to kill some of Turnus's sleeping men, they were spotted by another troop of cavalry.

We saw their heads bobbing on spears in the distance. Turnus taunted the Trojans with them.

All that day we waited to fight, but Turnus entered the fort alone and killed hundreds of Trojans before diving into the river.

Nor did we fight the next day, for the Trojan leader had arrived with Arcadian and Etruscan forces. Turnus and some of our allies attacked them, and we waited for orders.

But we waited in vain.

﹡⟶

Camilla was as angry as a lioness. She paced up and down. "Why will Turnus not let us fight?" she demanded.

"Too many troops on the field cause confusion," the captain of Camilla's cavalry told us. "Some tribes are fighting for the Trojans and others for us, and it will be hard to tell who is our friend and who is our foe."

The fighting that second day was so savage that afterwards King Latinus sent a messenger to New Troy to ask for a truce to bury the dead. Everyone was surprised when the barbarian leader of the Trojans agreed.

Over the next few days messengers told us what was happening.

Back in Laurentum, King Latinus wanted to make peace with the Trojans. He wanted to give them his daughter in marriage after all!

Turnus had gone back to Laurentum to convince King Latinus not to trust the Trojans.

The last day of the truce came, and we thought we might never see action. But then a spy came with news. The Trojans and their allies were on their way to Laurentum!

"We must go there, too," Camilla's voice said, from inside our silk tent. "This time I will not wait until they summon me. I will go to Turnus and demand to fight."

As she came out, the four of us gasped.

For she had bared one breast, just like an Amazon!

17

WARRIOR QUEEN

With one breast bare, Camilla climbed onto her horse and rode out to her cavalry.

The roar that greeted her was like thunder.

"I have sent a messenger to Turnus in Laurentum," she cried. "Queen Camilla is coming to his aid with her brave, bronze-clad men of Privernum!"

They cheered again and we set off for Laurentum.

Magnificent Camilla rode before us.

Tulla and I rode behind on her left. Tarpi and Larina were on her right. Then came her 200 horsemen, ready to follow their warrior queen to the Underworld.

On the road, people came in from fields to stare. They gaped in wonder at Camilla's beauty and boldness.

As we neared Laurentum, a great cry arose from the people gathered on the town walls.

Turnus had just come out of the town gates. He was on foot, dazzling in his armour. When his men saw Camilla in gold and purple with one bare breast, their mouths hung open just like the villagers and farmers.

As she came closer, Turnus grinned. He tossed back his long black hair as a horse tosses its mane.

Camilla swung a leg over her horse's neck and slid to the ground. That was our signal. In one perfect movement, the four of us and the 200 horsemen followed her lead.

"Turnus!" Camilla said in her clear voice. "Let me and my troops prove our bravery by facing the enemy alone, while you and your men stay here to protect the town walls."

Turnus nodded. "Bold words!" he said, in a voice all could hear. "Worthy of a warrior queen. Since you have shown such courage, will you dare something even greater? My scouts have told me that enemy horsemen have been ordered to attack this town. Meanwhile, the Trojan leader and his foot soldiers are coming by a narrow mountain pass. They hope to surprise us by coming from two directions! There is a place where my men and I can wait in ambush for them."

"The glade of the God of Wine," I said in a low voice. Camilla nodded.

"Queen Camilla," Turnus went on, in a booming voice, "will you stay here and defend Laurentum against the enemy cavalry? I will leave you some of my captains, but you will be the commander."

Camilla lifted her chin. "My troops and I will be honoured," she said. "We will not let you down."

18

THE BATTLE FOR LAURENTUM

My first real battle was not what I expected.

It is one thing to ride backwards on a pony across an empty plain.

It is another to ride backwards when the air is full of flying arrows, javelins, dust and shouts.

It is one thing to fire arrows at a dummy stuffed with hay.

It is another to kneel beside a young man who is bleeding from your arrow in his neck.

It is one thing to see your friend throw a battle-axe with perfect aim and hit a charcoal target on a wall.

It is another to see her striking a youth who is begging for mercy. To see brains mixed with blood ooze out of the eye sockets of his helmet.

To see the look of joy on her face as she turns to meet the next foe.

Camilla was born for battle.

We were not.

I saw Larina and Tulla cowering at the edge of the field, at the foot of Pluto's Hill, where we had danced that spring. Larina's horse lay dying and they were weeping over her. Tarpi still fought on, but her face was as white as the moon and she swung her axe at friend and foe alike.

Then one of my arrows hit an enemy horseman, more by luck than skill. I was still bending over him when I felt a searing pain in my leg. A javelin had grazed me. I cried out and tried to stand, the poor boy at my feet forgotten.

An arrow sneered past my cheek.

A man screamed.

A thunder of hoof beats told me a horse was about to trample me into the dust.

I turned to meet death face on, in case Camilla was watching.

The rider bearing down on me was not an enemy. It was Tarpi.

Her strong arms lifted me up and onto her horse.

They opened the town gates for us, then barred them again as fast as they could.

"Where are you taking me?" I gasped, as we rode up one of the deserted streets.

"To my house," she said, "to bind your wounds."

"That can wait!" I cried. "Take me up to the wall. I need to see the battle."

We turned back and slid off the horse. Tarpi helped me limp up the stone stairs to the crowded town wall. People made way for us, patting us both on the back. I was hardly aware of it.

I had to know if Camilla was still alive.

19

DEATH OF A WARRIOR

How can I describe the battle as I saw it from above?

It was like threads on a loom, with friends and enemies woven into one dense mass.

It was like stew in a pot, bits of men stirred together with spears and axes and swords.

It was like the waves of the sea when they beat against the rocks of the shore.

The battle field was the shore.

The town walls and ditch were the rocks.

The warriors were the waves.

Tarpi held me up while an old woman bound my leg with strips of linen.

Below us the warriors swirled towards us and then rushed back again.

I saw Camilla at once. Like a seagull bobbing on the waves.

Three times our side advanced against the enemy horsemen.

When we attacked, she was always near the front, waving her axe or tossing javelins.

When we were in retreat, Camilla rode backwards and fired silver arrows at the enemy.

Then at last the warriors crashed together in man-to-man combat.

As I looked down upon the battle, I tried to do what Camilla had taught me. I tried to see with one hundred Argus eyes. But I could not do it. I could not take my eyes from her.

I saw her hair flash, her cape flutter and her white horse rear.

It was her first battle, but they tell me that she killed twelve men. Twelve!

One man came with his chest bare, like hers. She speared him in his naked torso and he fell from his horse to the ground. In agony, he chewed the bloody dust and twisted on her spear.

Still on her horse, Camilla tugged the spear from his body. She was just in time to face two new attackers. She used the bloody spear to kill them both.

Next a man in a wolf skin attacked her. She used the gory spear to end his life, too. I saw her lips move as she taunted him, but I could not hear her words.

When a warrior on a black horse chased her, she spurred her white mare and was soon chasing him. She used her bronze axe to split his head like a walnut in its shell. I covered my eyes, and when I parted my fingers, I saw a young Etruscan on horseback. He was pointing at the ground. It was a challenge for her to fight him on foot.

I knew she could not hear me, but I still shouted, "No!"

When she leaped down to fight him, the coward wheeled his horse and galloped off! But he moved slowly on the crowded battle field while Camilla darted after him, as fast as a boar. She killed him with ease.

We cheered from the walls, our voices raw with joy.

A hand grabbed mine and I turned my head to see a lovely blonde girl beside me. "Camilla is so brave!" Princess Lavinia said. "I have just come from the Temple of Minerva," she told me. "My mother and I made offerings and prayed for all of you, but most of all for her."

I stared at Lavinia in wonder. Camilla had won even her heart.

But on my other side, Tarpi stiffened. "See that Etruscan," she said. "He has been following Camilla for the whole battle."

I looked where she pointed. I saw a warrior with a short black beard under his bronze helmet.

"You're right!" I cried. "He's hunting her."

"Oh no!" Lavinia grabbed my hand.

"Camilla! Watch out!" Tarpi and I screamed.

Camilla froze. In a swirl of chaos, she and her horse were the only things not moving.

Had she heard us?

Had she realised that a hunter had her in his sights?

No. Her gaze was fixed on a dazzling rider with a golden bow. He wore purple, red and yellow, and his golden helmet glittered in the sun.

Did Camilla want his clothing for herself? Or as a gift for the goddess Diana? I will never know.

We all saw the enemy's spear fly towards her. But Camilla did not.

She had forgotten her own rule of battle – Argus eyes.

The spear struck her bare breast.

I cried out, then pushed my way along the wall and down the stairs. I had to help her!

A wounded warrior on a grey horse had just come in the gate. As men helped him off, I jumped on the horse's back. I gasped with pain as I kicked my heels and rode into the battle again.

The air was full of dust and shouts, but some instinct steered me to her.

She was swaying on her mare, trying to pull out the spear, but its point was deep between her ribs.

I slid off and ran to her.

Camilla's white horse was red with her blood. As she slumped to one side I held her up.

"Acca?" she gasped.

"I am here, dear sister."

"It hurts. And everything is so dark. Is it dusk already?"

"Yes," I lied. "It is almost dusk."

Her head dropped forward. Then she lifted it. Her face was white as death.

"Acca!" she whispered. "You must find Turnus. Tell him to come now, or we are lost. That is my final command. And now, dear sister. Farewell."

I eased her to the ground. Larina, Tulla and Tarpi were beside me. They bent over her and their tears fell like hot rain.

But she was gone.

I saw her soul flutter out of her mouth and fly down to the Underworld.

For a moment the sounds of the battle faded. Then the four of us tipped back our heads and sent a cry of grief to the heavens above.

20

THE TROJAN LEADER

Camilla was dead.

I had to obey her last command. If I didn't, her sacrifice would be in vain.

Dizzy with pain, I mounted the grey stallion and urged him on to the forest and the hills beyond. I clung to his neck and hid my face in his mane. The battle was still raging all around us, but somehow we made it out alive.

At the first chance, I turned to look back at the plain. Camilla's death had made our side panic. The enemy had pushed us back to the very gates. Our soldiers were battling for their lives, as their wives and children watched from the ramparts above.

Then I saw something amazing. The women of Laurentum started to throw crude wooden spears down upon the enemy. Later I discovered they were made of looms they had taken apart. They had sharpened the points of the wooden beams and hardened them in the fire. The women had been inspired by Camilla's bravery.

And my mother was one of them!

But I knew I had to get help soon, or all would be lost.

I turned the grey horse and rode into the woods, taking the path the enemy would take. When I was close to the place where Turnus had set his trap the way became narrow and steep. No horse could climb that trail. I slid off him.

When I landed on the ground, the pain in my leg made me gasp.

For a moment the world spun around me. I sucked in air and forced myself to be strong.

Then I started up the path. Every step was a stab of fire.

When at last I came into the secret glade, I was covered with cold sweat.

I saw Turnus striding back and forth, his men in ranks behind him. He ran to me and gripped my arms, for I was about to faint.

"What is it?" he cried.

"My lord," I gasped. "Camilla is dead. Her last words were for you. She begged you to come to our aid. Our enemy are at the gates. If they enter, they will kill our men, rape our women and make slaves of our children. They will burn the town, the palace and the ancient grove."

"No!" Turnus lifted his face to the sky and bellowed like a bull. Then he pushed me away. "Back!" he cried to his men. "Back to Laurentum!"

The world around me grew dark. Was it dusk? Or was I dying, too?

I did not care. Without Camilla my life was nothing.

With dim eyes I saw Turnus lead his foot soldiers out of the glade and down the narrow path to the town. They would be in Laurentum in the time it takes to skin a deer.

When they had gone, I limped to the cliff. From here I could see Turnus's troops taking the south path. It was narrower but more direct.

No sooner were they out of sight than I heard the clink of armour and the footsteps of troops.

Soldiers appeared in the gully below. They wore leggings and long-sleeved tunics under their armour.

Trojans!

I groaned and clung to a silver birch.

If Turnus had waited, he could have defeated them there and then.

Then I saw their leader. He wore a short red cloak and carried his helmet under one arm. He was very handsome, almost beautiful. His curly brown hair was shot with silver and his eyes were sad.

Just as I had recognised Camilla, I knew this man was their leader, the "Pirate".

And one look at his face told me the truth – he did not want this war.

Turnus wanted it. Queen Amata wanted it. My friends and I wanted it. Perhaps even the gods wanted it.

But I could see that the Trojan leader was sick of it.

And so were his men.

A terrible idea came into my head.

What if the death of Silvia's deer had simply been a terrible accident?

What if Lavinia really should marry this sad and beautiful man?

What if we were wrong and they were right?

That would mean Camilla's death was for nothing.

The trees started to spin around me.

When the darkness came, it was a mercy.

21

THE STATUE OF CAMILLA

Ten years have passed since Camilla died in battle.

I am standing with three of my dearest friends and our children in the shady woods near Privernum. The woods smell of dry grasses and cork bark. The hot air throbs with insects and I can hear the clank of goat bells from the rocky hills near by.

We are looking at a painted marble statue on a grassy burial mound. The statue shows a young woman on horseback. Her hands grip the bronze spear buried in her right breast.

"Did it hurt?" a curly-haired boy asks. His name is Silvius and he is not quite nine years old.

"It hurt terribly," his mother, Queen Lavinia, whispers. "And it killed her."

"Was she an Amazon?" Tarpi's seven-year-old daughter asks in a clear voice.

"She was as brave as an Amazon," Tarpi says. "But she was a Latin, like us. She fought to save us from the Trojans."

"The Trojans? But Father is a Trojan!" Larina's son says.

"Yes," Larina replies. "We all married Trojans in the end."

"All but Tulla," I say, and my voice is soft.

Tulla is the only one not with us today. She truly loved Turnus and she refused to marry a Trojan, even after they had shown themselves to be kind and brave. She would have nothing to do with us again. For Lavinia had married their leader – the man who finally ended the war when he killed Turnus in single combat.

"What was her name?" Tarpi's little girl asks. She is still looking at the statue.

"Her name was Camilla." Tarpi chokes back a sob and I feel my own eyes prick with tears.

"Like you!" Prince Silvius turns to my daughter.

My Camilla is almost nine, with straight dark hair like me and smiling grey eyes like her Trojan father.

"Yes." My daughter nods. "I was named Camilla after her."

"Did you know her, Aunt Acca?" Prince Silvius asks. He has the same clear grey eyes as his father, the Trojan Leader.

"Yes," I whisper. "We all knew her. We all fought at her side."

"All except me." Queen Lavinia bites her lower lip.

"And the rest of us hardly at all," says Larina. "She was the only real warrior among us."

"But you all have a fighting spirit," Lavinia says.

"So do you, my Queen," I tell her.

Tarpi nods. "Those girlish Trojan men needed to mix their blood with us manly Latin women."

"Papa's not girlish!" Tarpi's little girl protests. "And you're not manly."

We all smile. Tarpi has a baby boy at her breast.

My own Camilla tilts her head to one side. "Mama, if Camilla died trying to save you and your friends from the Trojans but you ended up marrying them, does that mean her death was in vain?"

For a moment there is no sound but the throb of crickets.

It is a question I have asked myself many times.

"No," I say at last. "Her death was not in vain. She taught us to be brave. And to fight for what we believe. She won the greatest prize a leader can win, the respect and love of her people."

"The reward of bravery," Larina says, "is eternal glory."

I go up to the statue and I rest my hand on her marble arm.

"Dear Camilla," I say in a clear voice. "A spear saved you when you were little. And one took your life when you were in the flower of your youth. We will never forget you, dear sister. Rest in peace."

Before I turn to go back down, the goddess Diana shows me an image in my head. I see a baby tied to a spear, floating above a raging torrent. It is a moment held in time, like a bee in amber.

And I see that baby Camilla is not crying, but laughing with delight.

ABOUT CAMILLA – A NOTE FROM THE AUTHOR

Queen of the Silver Arrow is based on the story of Camilla by the Roman poet Virgil, but there are many gaps in his story and I had to use my imagination to fill these in. If you read Books 7 and 11 of Virgil's epic poem *The Aeneid* you will find out which bits of *Queen of the Silver Arrow* are in his original story.

CAROLINE LAWRENCE has written lots of exciting novels set in ancient times, including …

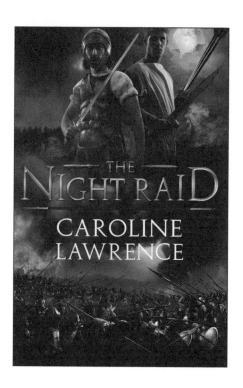

They say when someone stabs you it doesn't hurt. They say it feels like a fist has punched you. That you hardly notice it, in the heat of battle. They are wrong.

The night Troy fell, Rye and Nisus ran for their lives. Nisus left his family behind. Rye could not save his father.

Now the survivors of Troy have come to a new land and their leader has gone to seek allies to help their cause. When their new home comes under attack, Rye and Nisus see a chance to win back their honour.

www.barringtonstoke.co.uk